Orphaned Beluga

Susan Hughes

Cover by Susan Gardos
Illustrations by Heather Graham

SCHOLASTIC CANADA LTD.
Toronto New York London Auckland Sydney
Mexico City New Delhi Hong Kong Buenos Aires

Scholastic Canada Ltd.
175 Hillmount Road, Markham, Ontario L6C 1Z7, Canada
Scholastic Inc.
555 Broadway, New York, NY 10012, USA
Scholastic Australia Pty Limited
PO Box 579, Gosford, NSW 2250, Australia
Scholastic New Zealand Limited
Private Bag 94407, Greenmount, Auckland, New Zealand
Scholastic Ltd.
Villiers House, Clarendon Avenue, Leamington Spa,
Warwickshire CV32 5PR, UK

"Baby Beluga"
Words by Raffi, D. Pike. Music by Raffi.
©1980 Homeland Publishing (SOCAN),
a divison of Troubadour Music Inc.
All rights reserved. Used by permission.

National Library of Canada Cataloguing in Publication
Hughes, Susan, 1960-
    Orphaned beluga / Susan Hughes ; illustrated by Heather Graham.
(Wild paws ; 4)
ISBN 0-439-98986-8

1. White whale—Juvenile fiction. 2. Animal rescue—Juvenile fiction.
I. Graham, Heather, 1959- II. Title. III. Series: Hughes, Susan, 1960- Wild
paws ; 4.

PS8565.U42O76 2004   jC813'.54   C2003-905220-6

6 5 4 3 2 1   Printed in Canada   04 05 06 07 08

To Heather Tamminem

Thank you to Sylvain De Guise, a veterinarian in the Department of Pathobiology at the University of Connecticut who has studied beluga whales for years. This story is based on his real-life rescue of an upriver beluga whale in Canada, and I appreciate his assistance in providing me with some of the authentic details.

Contents

Chapter One

Grandma's News

Max set down the bucket of water. She unzipped her spring jacket.

"Whew," she said to her friend Sarah, with a grin. "It's finally getting warm!"

Sarah smiled back. "Springtime! And I think Nutcracker likes it too. Look at him!"

Nutcracker was a red squirrel, and a permanent resident of the Wild Paws and Claws Clinic and Rehabilitation Centre. His pen had been built around two small trees. The tops of the trees just touched the wire roof. Nutcracker was lying on one of the branches in the sunshine, sound asleep.

"I don't think I've ever seen him when he wasn't

awake and complaining about something," Max said.

Sarah took out Nutcracker's water dish, poured out the puddle on its bottom and refilled it with fresh water from her bucket. Max did the same for Bandit and Flora. At first, she couldn't spot the two raccoons. Then she noticed that Flora was curled up in the corner of the enclosure. But where was Bandit?

Max stood for a minute and scanned the pen more closely. Ah, *there* was Bandit. The raccoon had spent most of the winter snug in the hollow tree that stood in the corner of the pen. But today Bandit, like Nutcracker, was enjoying the warm rays of the sun. He was lounging on one of the branches at the far side of the tree.

Max sighed happily. It gave her a good feeling to know that the animals were safe and content. Abigail Abernathy, the owner of Wild Paws and Claws, took good care of them. Max and Sarah did their best to help out too.

Max and her family had moved to the village of Maple Hill late last spring. She had learned about Wild Paws and Claws after finding a helpless baby bobcat in the woods. After leaving the tiny kitten at the clinic, Max had been worried and anxious about her. At school, Sarah had listened carefully to Max's story. Sarah was an animal lover too, and she and Max had become instant best friends. Now they were both regular volunteers at the centre.

"Done," Sarah called out.

"Me too," Max said. The two girls went to the utility shed to put away their buckets.

"Want to come over for lunch?" Max asked Sarah.

"Sure," Sarah said.

"Let's just tell Abbie that we're finished." The girls ran to the Wild Paws office and into the small messy room that was Abigail Abernathy's headquarters.

Abbie sat behind a desk piled high with papers and files. She peered at Max and Sarah through her round glasses. She had a pencil stuck behind her ear, and a carrot top poked out of her shirt pocket. Max knew the leftover vegetable would end up as a treat for one of the raccoons later in the day.

"Yes, girls?"

"We fed and watered all the animals and birds," Max told her. "We're leaving now, but we might be back tomorrow."

Abbie shook her finger at Max and Sarah and pretended to scold them. "You girls," she said. "Take a break! Take a day off! You've been here almost ten days in a row. You need a holiday!"

Sarah and Max laughed. Abbie knew they loved

coming to look after the animals. They didn't even think of it as work.

The girls headed down the long, stony driveway, chatting cheerfully. When they reached the gate and the sign that announced Wild Paws and Claws Clinic and Rehabilitation Centre, they turned onto Hare Bell Lane. Several minutes later, they had reached the edge of their village.

As the girls approached the small house that Max's family shared with the girl's grandmother, Max saw Grandma working in the front garden. She was wearing a straw hat and a spring jacket, and was raking last autumn's dead leaves off the flower-beds. Grandma turned and saw the girls, and instantly a huge smile spread across her face.

"Max! Sarah! Guess what?" she called.

The girls looked at one another. Grandma had put down the rake and was coming toward them. Her hands were fluttering excitedly. Max and Sarah hurried up the walkway to hear the news.

The spring sunshine lit up Grandma's rosy cheeks. "I had a phone call from my dear old friend Dr. Alain Leduc this week. He lives in Quebec. He studies beluga whales there."

Max nodded. She remembered hearing Grand-ma's stories about Dr. Leduc. He and Grandma both loved animals. Long ago they had become close pals just like Max and Sarah.

Grandma turned to Sarah. "Belugas look like large, chubby white dolphins. Do you remember the children's song?"

Sarah nodded as Grandma launched into the tune. *"Baby beluga in the deep blue sea . . ."* She sang loudly and slightly off key. Max and Sarah glanced at each other and tried not to giggle.

Then the girls joined in for a moment. *"Swim so wild, and you swim so free . . ."*

Max grinned. "I've seen pictures of belugas. They're really cute! They have small, bulgy heads and little eyes. In the photos I've seen, they sometimes look like they're smiling."

Grandma nodded. "That's them, all right."

Max's brow wrinkled. "But your friend lives in Quebec. How can he study belugas there? Don't they live up in the Arctic Ocean?"

"You're quite right," Grandma agreed, looking proudly at Max. "Most beluga whales *do* live in the Arctic Ocean. They often swim in the shallow waters near the coast. But there are some that live in the St. Lawrence River, which flows through Quebec. My friend studies the St. Lawrence belugas." Her eyes sparkled. "And guess what? Alain has invited me to

5

come for a visit — and to see these special whales!"

Max's brown eyes grew wide. "Oh, Grandma, you're so lucky! I've never seen a beluga whale. I've never seen *any* kind of whale!"

"Me neither," said Sarah. "Not in real life!" She twirled the end of one of her braids.

Max could just picture it. What a thrill it would be to look out over the water and see beluga whales swimming past, wild and free, just like the song said!

"Well, I *do* want to go," Grandma said slowly, looking at Max, "but I'm not sure that I will . . . unless you and Sarah agree to come with me." Grandma beamed with pleasure.

Max's mouth dropped open. She turned to Sarah, who could only stare back at her, speechless.

"Girls, I've already run it by your parents. They took a few days to think about it, but they've finally agreed to let you both come. I'll take good care of you every step of the way." Grandma grinned. "So what do you say? Do you want to come and learn about the whales close up?"

When Max and Sarah could finally speak, only one word came to their lips. "Yes!" they blurted out.

Chapter 2

Up in the Air

Sarah and Grandma switched seats so that Sarah could look out the window. "Oh, Max," she sighed. "I wish you could look! I can see right below the wing of the airplane. There are lakes and rivers. They look like glistening blue jewels. I wonder if we're already flying over Quebec. It's so beautiful."

Max shook her head. "Sorry," she said. "Maybe later."

Max had warned Sarah that she was nervous about flying. They had been in the air for an hour, and Max had relaxed a little. But she wasn't ready to look out the window yet.

Still, she was happy to be on her way to see the

belugas. She was so excited she could hardly breathe. She pulled some books from the knapsack at her feet.

"Let's talk some more about belugas," Max suggested, handing Sarah one of the books. Sarah nodded.

Max and Sarah had been very busy all week. They had worked extra hard at Wild Paws and Claws to make up for the time they would be away. And they had tried to get ahead in their schoolwork. There hadn't been much time to find out about beluga whales.

Sarah gazed at the pages of the book. "Listen to this." She began reading aloud: *"The beluga whale is a warm-blooded mammal. It has thick skin and a thick blubber coat. Blubber is fat. Up to forty percent of a beluga may be blubber. The blubber helps keep the beluga warm as it swims in the icy Arctic waters."*

Max pointed further down the page. "It says here that belugas like shallow water best because they feed on fish and other animals that live on the floor of the sea. But the Arctic ice sometimes forces the belugas into deep, open water in the winter."

Max showed Sarah the map of North America on the next page. The winter locations of belugas were marked on it in blue. Their summer locations were marked in red.

Max read the caption underneath the map, "*In the summer, belugas head for the mouths of rivers where the water is shallow. In the Arctic, they sometimes have to migrate hundreds of kilometres through the ice to get there.*"

"Alain told me that belugas sometimes swim right up Arctic rivers," Grandma chimed in. "They do that when they're hunting for fish, like salmon."

"The belugas we're going to see live in the St. Lawrence River." Max pointed to the large river on the map that flowed into Quebec from the east. It was marked in blue and red. "They live there all year-round." Then she added, "The caption here reads, *There are only about 500 belugas in the St. Lawrence River.*"

Sarah reached into her own knapsack and pulled out another book. "I got this yesterday," she told Max. "I only had time to flip through it, but I saw a great picture." She opened the book to a large underwater photograph that covered both pages.

Max smiled when she saw the image of an adult and a baby beluga whale.

"Look, the adult whale is white and the baby whale is pinkish-brown," Sarah pointed out. "Listen to this: *Females give birth every three years. Their babies are called calves. When the calf is born, it is pink or pinkish-brown. It is about 1.5 metres long, the height of a teenager. As the calf grows, its colour changes to a dark grey. Over the next few years, the whale becomes a lighter grey. By the time the whale is six or seven years old, it has turned white. Belugas can live for thirty years or more.*"

"Amazing," said Max.

The time passed quickly. Before they knew it, the pilot was asking them to do up their seatbelts for landing. Max clicked her seatbelt closed. She leaned over Grandma and looked out Sarah's window.

"Oh, wow," she exclaimed. "That must be Quebec, and this must be the St. Lawrence River!"

A large blue river stretched out below her. She shivered with awe. She knew that the water she was looking at came directly from the Great Lakes and then flowed out to the Atlantic Ocean.

Sarah glanced at Max. She saw that her friend was no longer nervous about flying. They shared a smile.

In another few minutes, the plane was circling over the airport. Soon it had touched down.

After picking up their luggage from the revolving carousel, Max, Sarah and Grandma headed toward the airport lobby area.

"Now, Alain said that he'd meet us near the — "

Grandma didn't have time to finish her sentence. A large man with a silver beard had picked her up in a bear hug. Her feet dangled in the air.

"Beth! Beth! You haven't changed a bit!" boomed the man in a hearty voice.

"Ah, and Alain, neither have you. You are as sweet as ever!" Grandma answered, as the man put her gently back down on the ground. "It is so nice to see you. We are so excited to be here!"

Grandma introduced Max and Sarah to Dr. Leduc, and he squeezed their hands firmly.

"I am happy that Beth has brought you along. We'll have a wonderful time together — you, me and the belugas," he promised them. "Now come. My car is parked outside. We have to drive several hours to get to my home. Let me help you with your bags."

The travellers and Dr. Leduc piled into his small car and set off. As he drove, Dr. Leduc talked and talked. "We will relax this evening," he told them. "Then tomorrow we will see if we can spot some of my whales." He looked at the girls in the rearview mirror. "I know they're not really mine. They are wild whales. But because I study them — because I spend so much time thinking about them, learning about them and worrying about them, I call them *my* whales. I'm sure you understand."

Max nodded. She had helped Abbie rescue several wild animals. Even though they were being returned to the wild, she always felt a bond with them. She knew the animals didn't belong to her. It was a *feeling* that connected her to them. It was the feeling that made them "her" animals.

"So tomorrow we will get up and go to the river. We will go for a ride in my small boat. We'll try to find the pod of whales that I have been studying most recently. A pod is a small group." Dr. Leduc added, "It's not definite that we will find the whales. They keep on the move, so we can't always meet up with them. But you never know. We might be lucky!"

"That sounds just terrific," Grandma said. She turned and looked at the girls. "What do you two think?"

"Great!" said Max.

But Sarah didn't speak. Max glanced over at her. Sarah was pale and her lips were pressed together.

"Sarah?" Max asked. "Are you all right?"

To Max's concern, Sarah shook her head. "There's one little problem," she said softly. "*I'm* afraid of boats. I was hoping we could see the belugas from shore."

Chapter 3

Searching for Belugas

"Oh, Sarah, that's OK," Max said. "I was afraid of airplanes, but I flew today. And it wasn't so bad."

Sarah nodded slowly. "You're right," she agreed. "You did." Then she began to blush. "But I'm not a great swimmer . . ."

Max nudged Sarah's arm playfully. "Well, you'll just have to wear a life jacket tomorrow. You'll do fine."

Dr. Leduc had overheard from the front seat. "Your friend is correct, Sarah," he said. "We must all wear life jackets. It's the only way to stay safe, even for the best of swimmers." He nodded. "You know, it is nice to see the whales from shore — and most people *should* see them that way. But our studies make it essential to observe them from a boat. We need to be close up to see their markings and tell them apart. We follow very strict rules, making sure we go slowly and then stop when we see them. We treat the whales with great respect. You won't be sorry if you come and see a beluga close up."

By the time they arrived at the little village where Dr. Leduc lived, it was evening. He pulled up in front of a white bungalow on the banks of the river. Tired and hungry, the three travellers went up to their rooms to unpack. Max and Sarah phoned home to report that they had arrived safely.

After a delicious dinner, Dr. Leduc took them on a short walk around the village. When they met one of his neighbours, the girls said *bonjour*, which is French for hello.

Max had thought that she would be too excited to sleep that night, but she didn't even remember closing her eyes after her head hit the pillow. The next thing she knew, the sunshine was pouring through the bedroom window, and it was time for breakfast.

Everyone ate quickly. "Dress warmly," Dr. Leduc warned his guests. "It will be very cold on the water."

Max and Sarah had each packed a wool sweater,

snow pants, a winter jacket, a hat and mittens. After hearing Dr. Leduc's words of advice, they decided to wear everything.

And as they stepped off the dock and into the small observation boat, they were glad they had. The cold wind whistled past them as it swept over the waves of the St. Lawrence River.

"Friends, meet my research assistants, Sylvie and Claude. Sylvie will be joining us today. Claude will be staying behind to do some record keeping," said Dr. Leduc.

"*Bonjour*," they all said. Both Sylvie and Claude wore yellow waterproof jackets and overalls and big black gloves and boots.

"Here are your life jackets," said Sylvie. She helped Max and Sarah buckle up the orange life jackets. Max was grateful for the extra warmth the bulky jacket gave her. She glanced over at Sarah. Her friend's eyes looked even bluer than usual. Her teeth were chattering.

"Cold?" Max asked her.

"Cold — and nervous," Sarah admitted. She gripped her orange life jacket with both hands, then smiled. "I'll be all right."

Grandma nodded. "Yes, you'll be just fine," she reassured her.

"OK, we're off!" sang out Dr. Leduc from inside the cabin. He was at the wheel of the boat. "Why don't you come inside out of the wind and sit down until we get close to where the whales might be?"

Max and Sarah followed Grandma into the cabin. They sat together on a cushioned bench and looked excitedly out the window. Sylvie untied the two ropes. Claude helped push the boat away from the dock. Dr. Leduc pressed down on a lever, and the boat surged forward.

Dr. Leduc had to raise his voice to be heard over the hum of the engine. "We've been coming to watch the belugas for many months," he explained to his guests. "One of our goals is to try to take photos of the belugas so that we can tell them apart. This way, we can study them and learn more about their behaviour."

Sylvie sat down beside them. "The beluga's scientific name, *Delphinapterus leucas,* means 'white dolphin without a fin,'" she said. "That's because belugas have only a hard ridge on their back, not a fin – unlike most other whales."

"Is there a reason for that?" Max asked.

Sylvie smiled. "Good question." Then she explained, "Belugas sometimes swim under the ice.

17

But they need to come to the surface to breathe. Scientists think that the hard ridge on the beluga's back, called the dorsal ridge, comes in handy then. The whale can use it to break through ice as thick as ten centimetres!"

"Wow!" Max said.

"So, is the dorsal ridge one of the ways to tell the belugas apart?" Sarah asked.

"Yes, that's right! We have identified over two hundred different belugas now," Sylvie said proudly. "We give them names too," she added. "Like Marshmallow, Maple, Alpha and Vitesse." Sylvie turned back to the boat cabin window. Her eyes scanned the surface of the wide river.

"I like the name Marshmallow," Max said to Sarah with a grin. Sarah smiled back. She didn't look quite as pale or worried about being out on the water. The boat was moving quickly, but the ride was not too bumpy and they could still see the distant shore.

"Belugas live in groups, or pods," Dr. Leduc said. "They travel along certain routes from one area to another. Knowing the routes gives us a better chance of finding them."

"Although we don't seem to be having much luck today," Sylvie added.

"Ah, well, it's just nice to be out here, enjoying the fresh air," Grandma said cheerfully.

Dr. Leduc drove on slowly for several hours. They went to three places where he thought they might come across the beluga pod he knew best. Each time, he stopped the boat and everyone stood out on the deck and silently watched the water for any sign of movement.

The fourth time they stopped, Max and Sarah were the first to hurry onto the deck. Even though it was chilly, Max loved the feel of the wind blowing

against her cheeks. The sun was shining, the sky was blue and she was excited to be out on the mighty St. Lawrence River. The boat bobbed up and down on the waves, and Max and Sarah held on to the rail to keep their balance. They couldn't see very far below the surface of the shifting water.

"It's almost impossible to believe that there is so much life down there — plants, fish, clams and even belugas," Max said to Sarah. "It's like a whole other world!"

Together they gazed out at the water. They hoped and waited, but there was no sign of any whales.

At last, Dr. Leduc poked his head out of the cabin. "Well, I guess we'll head back. I'm sorry, girls." He lifted his hands. "We cannot control the wild things. They do as they please, not as we wish." Dr. Leduc, Sarah and Grandma headed back into the cabin, and Sylvie put the cap back on her camera.

Max took one last look out at the river. A shadow darkened the water beside the boat — a bird flying by, Max guessed. She glanced up at the sky to see what kind it was.

There was no bird.

Max's heart began to pound. She turned to the river and gripped the rail. Her eyes searched the water's surface, back and forth.

And then there it was. It wasn't the shadow of a bird. It wasn't the shadow of anything. It was a dark shape underwater, and as Max watched, still as a statue, it lifted to the air and broke the surface. It was a white beluga, and it was grinning right at her!

Chapter 4

The Sea Canaries

For a minute, Max did nothing. She could only grin back at the amazing animal.

The beluga's head was right out of the water. It was smooth and round, and it bulged at the top. The beluga had a very short beak and rubbery lips. They curled up at the edges into what seemed like a smile!

Then Max heard Sylvie's voice beside her. She listened to the research assistant without taking her eyes off the beluga.

"This is Coco. We call him that because he is a bit of a clown. He is very curious about our boat — and about us."

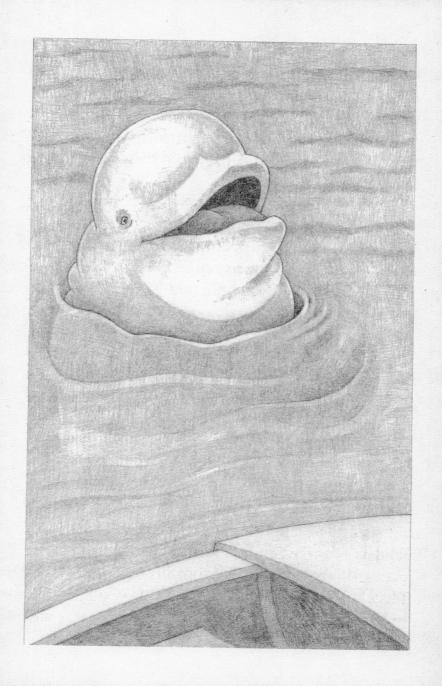

Sarah had returned from the cabin right away to stand next to Max. She laughed softly. "Oh, Max, isn't he sweet?" she asked.

Max gazed at Coco, enchanted by his grinning face. He was so close! A real, wild beluga — right in front of her!

"When whales do this" — Sylvie pointed at the whale — "when they lift their heads above the water and watch what is happening on the surface, it is called *spyhopping*," she explained.

"I understand," Max said, nodding. "Hopping up above the water, and spying on us. Spyhopping!"

Just then, Coco seemed to have spied enough. He blinked, ducked his head and, with a flip of his tail, dove out of sight.

"Oh," Sarah said with a sigh.

But a moment later, Max and Sarah gasped with delight. There were two more white shapes slipping by underwater!

"Look," Sylvie said, pointing. "More members of Coco's pod."

"And there are others," Max cried. Three more belugas swam by, and the trio broke the water's surface with their backs. Max could see their dorsal ridges.

"Belugas are mammals. Like us, they breathe air,"

Sylvie said. "They have to come to the surface of the water to breathe. They take in air through the blow-hole, which is just behind their forehead. When they are swimming, they come to the surface to breathe several times a minute."

Suddenly the quiet air was filled with a strange clucking sound. The sound grew louder, and then was joined by barking, trills and yaps!

"What *is* that?" Sarah asked.

Dr. Leduc and Grandma were standing near the back of the boat. Dr. Leduc grinned and gestured to Max and Sarah. The girls quickly made their way over and saw that six more belugas were swimming nearby.

"Belugas are called sea canaries because of their many songs!" Dr. Leduc explained. "In fact, only we humans make more different kinds of sounds than beluga whales."

"My gracious," Grandma said. Her face was lit with pleasure. "How do they do that?"

"The beluga makes sounds in its air passage, and then forces the air out through its blow hole," Dr. Leduc said. "The whale can change the sounds it makes by changing the shape of its air passages and, likely, its melon. That's the name we use for the bulge on the beluga's forehead."

Max listened to the whales, spellbound. "It's almost as if they are talking to one another," she said.

"Yes, we believe they *do* use some sounds to communicate with one another," said Dr. Leduc. "Other sounds help them navigate, and this is called echolocation. Belugas make a 'click' noise as they swim. They use their melon to aim the sounds. When the sound bounces off something and comes back to them, they can tell the size and shape of the object. It lets them know if there's an obstacle in the way – or some fish for dinner!"

Now everyone was silent. It was a moment for watching and listening.

Max took in the sight of the three long white whales moving gracefully through the water. She could tell them apart: one had a scar above its left fin, one had a curved dorsal ridge and one had a droopy right eye.

The two younger belugas were darker, pudgy and full of spunk. One bumped into the other. Was it on purpose or an accident? Max grinned. Were they playing a game?

The sixth whale was the longest of all. It may have been living in these waters for over thirty whole years. That was about three times as long as Max had been alive!

Max hugged herself happily. She had never imagined that they would get such a close look at the whales. She never thought they'd look right back at her – or that she'd hear them sing!

Then, as suddenly as the belugas had come, they vanished. The canary songs faded. All that was left was the sound of the wind and the waves.

Max grabbed Sarah's arm. "Can you believe it? We just saw belugas!"

"It was *so* amazing," Sarah replied. "It was definitely worth coming out on a boat!"

The boat ride back to the dock was long, but the girls sat happily, riding the waves and chatting about Coco and the other grinning belugas. At midday, Max finally felt the boat turn and then slow. Sylvie prepared to tie up to the dock.

But then Max heard Dr. Leduc say, "What is this? What's wrong?"

She looked up to see Claude, Dr. Leduc's other research assistant, on the dock. He was frantically waving his arms and shouting. Max couldn't hear anything he was saying over the sound of the boat's motor. But she could see the look on Claude's face and she knew what it meant.

Something was wrong.

Chapter 5

An Emergency

"Dr. Leduc! Dr. Leduc! There is an emergency!"

Now Max could hear Claude's urgent voice. The boat was close to the dock, and Claude was reaching for the rope that Sylvie had thrown to him.

Dr. Leduc cut the engine. He hurried out of the cabin as Claude pulled the boat over to the dock. Sylvie stepped out and tied one of the ropes to the dock.

"What is it?" Dr. Leduc's voice was calm, but he looked ready for anything.

Claude tied the other rope and gave a pull to make sure it was firm. He stood up. "There was a call while you were out," he said. "A young beluga whale is in danger. There is a dam being built across the water at St. Paul's River and he is upriver of it. If he doesn't head back down the river to the St. Lawrence soon, he will be trapped there by the dam."

Dr. Leduc didn't need to hear any more. "Let's get ready at once," he directed.

Sylvie sprang into action. She hurried to help Max, Sarah and Grandma take off their life jackets. She stashed them in a large bin on the boat.

As Dr. Leduc took off his own life jacket, he asked, "Who phoned you about this?"

"A local woman, Marie Blanc. She and her husband live near the river. They've been really interested in watching the young whale," Claude answered. "They knew the dam was being built, but they only found out this morning that the frame of the dam will be completed in a day or two. They called us immediately. They realized that the whale would be trapped, and they knew he wouldn't be able to permanently survive in the river."

Dr. Leduc nodded, deep in thought.

Then he turned to Grandma, Max and Sarah. "I'm sorry that this will interfere with our plans here," he said.

"Oh, Alain," Grandma replied. "It's an emergency. A whale in danger is much more important than our holiday here with you. And we've already seen so much today!"

"Well, what I'm wondering is whether I could have your help in this emergency." Dr. Leduc's blue eyes sparkled. "Will you come with us to help save this young whale? The more help we have, the better!" He tugged on his silver beard as he waited for their answer.

Grandma gave Max and Sarah a questioning look. "Girls?"

"Of course we want to come and help," Max replied, her heart thumping. "Right, Sarah?"

Sarah nodded vigorously. "Right," she said firmly. "Of course we do."

Dr. Leduc gave them a grateful thumbs-up. "Then we need to move right away. The river is four or five hours away by car." He glanced at his watch. "It is already past one. We will head back to the house, gather some clothes and have a quick lunch."

Grandma nodded. "Leave that to me."

Dr. Leduc turned to his assistants. "I need you both to come, too. Please take the other research truck, with the stretcher and inflatable boat. We may need all our rescue equipment."

Max's felt her stomach twist. How would they move the beluga? She hoped it would survive.

"OK, let's go," said Dr. Leduc.

Max, Sarah, Grandma and Dr. Leduc jumped into his car. They drove from the river's edge directly to Dr. Leduc's home. While Max and Sarah rushed up to their room to pack, Grandma took over in the kitchen.

"I can't believe it," Sarah said as she emptied out her dresser drawer. "So much is happening so quickly."

"I know," Max agreed. Her mind went straight to the beluga. She tried to picture it. What colour would a beluga calf be? Grey, perhaps. She wondered how big it would be. She hoped its mother was nearby.

The girls hurried downstairs with their bags. Grandma had made a tall stack of sandwiches. She was setting out napkins, and Dr. Leduc was pouring milk into cups.

"Dig in, girls," he encouraged them. "You must be hungry after our adventure on the St. Lawrence this morning. And we have a long drive ahead of us."

After everyone had eaten, they set off.

Sarah kept cheerfully pointing out interesting sights. She read the French signs on the small shops in the villages they drove through. Max smiled and tried to enjoy the ride too, but she found it hard to think about anything except the young beluga swimming in the river, soon to be trapped.

Dr. Leduc spoke up. "Claude told me some more about the whale before we left. According to Marie Blanc, the young whale and its mother left the St. Lawrence River and headed up toward St. Paul's River several weeks ago." He shook his head. "Sometimes belugas will head up smaller rivers in search of food. It isn't common, though.

"Then a sad thing happened. The mother beluga died. No one is certain why. She was found on a beach just a few days ago."

Max's face fell. "But how will the baby survive without its mother?" she cried.

"Well, from what he has been told, Claude figures that the young whale will be two years old this summer. Calves usually stay with their mothers for two years. They nurse until they are about twenty months old. I think our young friend is old enough to catch its own food now," Dr. Leduc said.

Max pictured Coco and his sweet face. She pictured the other belugas swimming freely beside the observation boat. The thought of a beluga in danger was awful. The thought of an endangered beluga calf *without its mother* was even worse!

Chapter 6

Rivière-
Saint-Paul

A Small Splash

"There!" Dr. Leduc cried. His voice sounded tired. He had been driving for hours. "That must be St. Paul's River!"

Max looked out the window. Beside them, a river ran under a bridge that spanned the road. It flowed toward the St. Lawrence.

"There's the sign," Max said. "*Rivière-Saint-Paul* − St. Paul's River," she read.

As they drove north, Max noticed the river starting to narrow. "I know that belugas sometimes swim up small rivers looking for fish. But why would they *stay* up here?" she asked Dr. Leduc.

"I'm not sure. It is unusual," he answered. "This

river is quite rocky and has many sandbars. It's possible that the mother and her calf became hemmed in, but had lots of food around and didn't need to move out." He pulled at his beard for a moment. Then he added, "Now it is our job to convince the young fellow that it is time to go! Yes? *Oui?*"

"*Oui!*" Max agreed. And the sooner the better!

Not long after, Max saw signs of construction by the riverside. Large steel girders rose out of the water. "Look, Sarah! There!" Max cried. "That must be the dam."

Sarah leaned over to get a better look out Max's window. Two of the three sections of the dam had been filled in with concrete. When the middle was filled in tomorrow or the next day, the dam would be complete. The water would be stopped.

And the beluga would be trapped, Max thought. That is unless we can get it to swim past here, so that it can return to the St. Lawrence. How can we possibly do that? And can we do it soon enough? "Dr. Leduc, do you really think we can rescue this whale?" Max asked. She squeezed her hands together anxiously.

"Max, we'll do our best," Dr. Leduc promised. "It's hard to know anything for certain at this point. But when we see the whale and the river tomorrow,

34

we'll have a better idea of what is possible. I do know that we'll do all we can to help the young beluga return to his real home in the St. Lawrence River."

Max and Sarah sat back in their seats. Grandma suggested that they listen to some music for a little while. Another twenty minutes passed as the sounds of violins, pianos and flutes filled the car. Now it was twilight. The trees were like tall dark shadows. The river was a black ribbon.

Soon, they saw a T-junction ahead. Max spotted a sign that read: *Village de Rivière-St-Paul*. It had an arrow pointing down the connecting road.

"Ah," said Dr. Leduc. He pulled the car over to the side of the road and parked. "According to Claude's directions, this is where our young beluga friend has been hanging about. Should we try to see if we can spot him, even though it's getting quite dark?"

"Oh, yes!" Max cried immediately, unbuckling her seatbelt.

"Yes, yes," chimed in Sarah.

At once, the girls were out of the car. "It's so dark," Sarah complained. "It's too bad we don't have a flashlight. It's hard to see anything!"

Grandma and Dr. Leduc joined them. "It is difficult to see anything, Sarah," Grandma agreed, peering into the distance. "I think I can just see the other side, but it's hard to be sure in this dusky light."

Max could hardly tell where the water began and the night sky ended. Was it possible that there might be a beluga whale down there?

A cool wind blew off the river, and Max shivered. Grandma must have noticed, because right away she commanded, "OK, gang, back to the car. There's no point in us all catching cold here. We'll return tomorrow when it's lighter — and a little warmer."

As the others hurried back to the car, Max stood for a moment longer. She imagined how it might be to live in the water — to move with the flick of a tail, to rise to the surface for air and then to sink into the water again.

"Where are you?" she whispered into the night. "Where are you, baby beluga?"

She heard a small splash in the water. And she saw something. It was the hint of a shape, shadowy but glistening. It was there . . . and then it was gone. Was it the beluga?

Just in case, Max whispered into the night, "Don't worry. We'll be back tomorrow."

Chapter 7

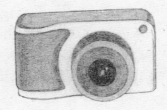

The Gymnast

When they reached the Blancs' home, Claude and Sylvie were already there.

The Blancs had kindly prepared a simple dinner for them, and they all ate around a large pine table. Mr. and Mrs. Blanc told them all about first spotting the mother and young whale a few weeks before. They told about hearing the sad news of the mother's death – and the alarming news about the dam.

Then Dr. Leduc and his assistants began to tell whale stories. They described their favourite whales. They shared the excitement of learning more and more about belugas. Max and Sarah listened, wide-eyed.

"Some people believe that belugas are as intelligent as people — or perhaps *more* intelligent," Sylvie said. "I once worked at a large aquarium. I sometimes swam with the belugas. They played with me and teased me. We made up games, and they understood the rules. They even made up their own rules! If only we could speak the same language as the belugas, I'm sure we would have a lot to teach one another."

Max nodded. She remembered the look in Coco's eyes. She remembered how the beluga had seemed to smile at her.

"Before I began working with Dr. Leduc," Claude explained, "I helped to count belugas on the St. Lawrence River. I think you know that the belugas on this river are endangered."

"The girls have read a little about it in their books. Could you tell us more?" asked Grandma.

Claude nodded. "The belugas on the St. Lawrence were hunted heavily for many years. Now they're being harmed by the pollution in the river. For a time, it looked like they might not survive. It is now illegal to hunt a beluga here, and there is a plan in place to keep track of the population of the St. Lawrence belugas and to take better care of them and their home, the river."

"So that's why counting them is so important,"

Max said. "To make sure they're doing OK."

"Yes," Claude agreed. "And right now, the population seems to be doing all right. There aren't many belugas – but the numbers don't seem to be dropping anymore." Then he grinned. "But counting whales isn't easy! We would go up in airplanes and take photos of the water. Later we would look at each photo and count the whales."

"But how could you take a photo of every whale in the whole St. Lawrence River?" asked Max.

"That would be impossible," Sarah said.

"You're right. We couldn't do that," Claude agreed. "What we had to do was to figure out how much of the river we *didn't* photograph. Then we had to guess how many whales we'd missed based on the number of whales we did see." Claude took a bite of cake and a sip of coffee. "Plus, it's even trickier than that. When we took a photo, there might be a whale there below the surface, but we wouldn't catch it on film. So we'd have to calculate that in as well. Just because we didn't see it didn't mean that it wasn't there."

"Wow," Max said. "That sounds complicated!"

Just then, Sarah gave a big yawn. She quickly tried to cover it up, but it was too late. Grandma had spotted her.

"Bedtime, girls!" she announced, getting up from the dinner table. "We've all had a busy day — and tomorrow will be just as adventurous."

Max and Sarah could hardly stay awake to talk about their exciting day of whale watching. As Max drifted to sleep on her cot, she remembered the splash in the river and the shape she thought she had seen. It felt like tomorrow would never come.

But then she opened her eyes, and it was morning. She had slept soundly all through the night. Excitement gripped Max. This was it: the day they would rescue the beluga! Max wakened Sarah, and the two girls jumped into their clothes and headed downstairs.

The others were already eating breakfast. "Come and have some toast or cereal," Mr. Blanc urged the girls. He placed more bowls and plates on the table. He poured juice into two cups.

Max smiled at him. "*Merci.*" She picked up a piece of toast and spread it with jam, but then could only nibble at it. She had suddenly had a troubling thought.

Sarah must have read her mind. "What if the work on the dam has already begun?" she asked. "What if the cement is being poured this morning?"

"Oh, girls, there was good news on the local radio channel before you came down," Grandma told them. "The workers will not begin the final stage of the dam until tomorrow." She clasped her hands together. "So we have arrived in time!"

A wonderful sense of relief swept over Max.

"Yes," Dr. Leduc agreed. "But the sooner we begin, the better. If we're not successful today . . ." He paused. "Well, it would nice to move the whale to safety as soon as possible."

Max nodded. She completely agreed. She put down her barely touched piece of toast.

"OK, everyone," Dr. Leduc announced. "Max and I think it's time to go and visit our young friend!"

Max and Sarah rode with Claude and Sylvie, and Grandma and the Blancs went with Dr. Leduc. They headed to the river, stopping in the same spot where they had parked the evening before.

The girls jumped out of the car. Max zipped up her jacket, breathing in the fresh spring air. She noticed that the river was quite shallow and there were many sandbars, just as Dr. Leduc had told them. It would be difficult for an animal as large as a whale to swim over them or find a way between them. No wonder the young whale was staying put.

He and his mother had gotten through somehow — but getting back out seemed tricky!

"Here is our little boat," Mrs. Blanc said. She pointed to an aluminum boat that was pulled up on the shore. "You may use it if you wish."

"Thank you," Dr. Leduc said. "But first, I must try to have a look at the beluga whale."

There had been no sign of it. The water was calm, flat and seemed absolutely empty of large mammals. But almost as soon as Dr. Leduc said the words "beluga whale," just like magic, there was a ripple on the water. And there was the young whale!

Max caught her breath as she saw him surface. The beluga's head didn't come out of the water, but the river was so clear, Max could see the animal perfectly. He had curious eyes and a grinning mouth, just like Coco. But this whale wasn't white like Coco. He was too young to be white yet. His skin was greyish. Max watched as the young whale's back rolled smoothly through the water, breaking the surface.

"Oh, he's lovely," whispered Sarah. "It's almost like he was waiting for us!"

The little beluga swam up the river in front of them, as if putting on a show. Then, just before he was out of sight, he turned and swam back. He wasn't as long as the young whales they had seen in the St. Lawrence River, but he was chubby like them. Max was enchanted. A baby beluga! Swimming wild and free!

The beluga turned and swam back alongside the riverbank, and then, when he reached a deeper spot, he somersaulted! Max and Sarah burst out laughing.

"Dolphins somersault a lot, but not belugas," said Claude. "That's really unusual. All in all, this is a very unpredictable calf!"

"He's a gymnast!" Sarah exclaimed, clapping her hands.

Max smiled. She had been so worried. She had imagined the whale lonely and scared, but instead he seemed full of spunk and spirit. She turned to the Blancs. "Have you given the beluga a name?" she asked. "Because I've just had a great idea. Could we call him Gymmy, because he is so gymnastic?"

Mrs. Blanc grinned. "That sounds fine to me," she said.

"Great idea," Sarah agreed. "Gymmy, the gymnastic beluga whale!"

Chapter 8

Go Away!

While Max, Sarah, Grandma and the Blancs enjoyed Gymmy's playful antics, Dr. Leduc and his assistants were examining him thoughtfully. Claude held a clipboard and a pen. He was writing down the scientist's observations.

"Gymmy looks to be about nineteen or twenty months old, as we thought. He is about two metres long, half what he will be when full grown. He looks quite healthy, not too skinny," Dr. Leduc reported. Claude wrote busily.

Gymmy swam past again. This time he seemed to nod, up and down, up and down. Sylvie laughed. "Other whales can't move their heads like that – up and down, or side to side," she marvelled. "Only belugas have such a flexible neck. And only belugas are so nosy!" she added.

Max smiled. It was obvious that Sylvie loved belugas very much.

Dr. Leduc looked through his binoculars to get a closer look at Gymmy. "Our friend is certainly swimming well, and he doesn't appear to have any wounds." He looked up at the others. "This is wonderful. It means he won't need to be flown to a rehabilitation facility. No, I think we can get the whale back to the St. Lawrence River ourselves."

Sylvie and Claude waited patiently as Dr. Leduc thought some more.

"OK," he said finally. "Here is what we will try. It will be difficult for us to get the Blancs' boat through the sandbars to the whale, but I think we can do it. I will go in the boat. But Sarah and Max, I would like your help." He looked at the two girls. "What do you say?"

A huge smile of surprise spread across Max's face. Sarah looked a little flushed, but she was smiling too.

"We'll try to drive Gymmy down the river," Dr. Leduc explained. "Hopefully, he'll be nervous about the sound of the engine. And Max and Sarah can bang the pipes that Claude has packed in the truck. When we make this big racket behind him, he should scoot right ahead of us in the direction of the St. Lawrence."

Claude disappeared. A moment later he returned with three life jackets and several metal pipes, which were about as long as his arm. He put the pipes in the boat.

Mr. Blanc and Grandma pushed the small boat partway into the water as Max, Sarah and Dr. Leduc put on their life jackets. Then the three rescuers climbed into the boat, and Mr. Blanc pushed them off.

With one pull of the starter rope, the boat engine started.

Carefully, Dr. Leduc nosed the little craft between the sandbars. Several times, Max could feel the bottom skim the top of the sandbars. But they didn't get stuck. Soon they had reached the deeper water where Gymmy was now playing. Almost immediately, the young whale came over to the boat.

"Look!" Max cried. "He's right here!" She was thrilled. Gymmy was so close, Max could almost touch him. He grinned at them as he swam alongside the slowly moving boat.

"OK, girls, we don't want Gymmy alongside us. We want him afraid of us. We want him to swim away — downstream and past the dam! So hold those pipes underwater and bang them. We won't hear the noise, but Gymmy will!" Dr. Leduc instructed.

Max and Sarah put the pipes underwater and began hitting them together. They even began to shout. "Go on!" they cried. "Go on, Gymmy! Go down that river! Off you go!"

Dr. Leduc yelled too. "Shoo! Shoo!" he shouted. "Go on!"

But the harder they tried to drive the whale, the more interested he became in them.

It almost made Max laugh. As she banged the pipes together, Gymmy turned his head and watched. It was as if he wondered why they were doing such an odd thing. It *must* look ridiculous, Max thought with a giggle. Two girls clanging pipes, shouting and yelling as loudly as they can — no wonder Gymmy was staring!

Finally Dr. Leduc slowed the motor. He signalled to the girls to stop their banging. "Maybe he'll come with us, if we can't seem to drive him ahead of us," he called to them over the sound of the motor. But as soon as the boat returned to the

sandbars, Gymmy turned around. He wanted to play. He wanted to frolic. He didn't seem to want to do anything difficult!

Dr. Leduc drove the boat to shore and turned off the engine. "Well, that didn't work."

"You two did a good job, though," said Sylvie, as Claude pulled the boat onto the beach. "You know, some whales just seem to like boats," she told them. "We're not sure why. Maybe they see boats as companions, as friends. They like to swim alongside them, in spite of the engine noise."

Sylvie was trying to sound reassuring, but Max had a sick feeling in her stomach. It hadn't worked. They hadn't rescued Gymmy. Now what? Would the young beluga be trapped forever?

Chapter 9

Whale on Board

"So now on to the next plan," Dr. Leduc said.

Max felt a glimmer of hope. There was another plan!

"OK, Sylvie, could you please go to the truck and get the hoop net and some extra rope? Then I'll need you to join me in the little boat with Max and Sarah. We'll try to capture the whale and bring him to shore." Dr. Leduc pointed. "We'll aim to land on that beach."

He took off his life jacket and then his jacket. Max saw that he was wearing a wet suit underneath.

"You look like you plan on going into the river!" Grandma joked.

Dr. Leduc answered, "That's *exactly* what I'm planning to do!"

Sylvie was back right away with the net and rope. Max could see that Sylvie and Claude were also wearing wet suits. "Come on, girls," Sylvie urged them. "You're really part of the team now. Hop back into the boat!" Once they and Dr. Leduc were seated in the motorboat, Sylvie started the engine and turned the boat toward the middle of the river. Max spotted Gymmy right away. He hadn't gone far. He must have been curious about all the activity.

In fact, as soon as the boat reached the deeper water, Gymmy swam right up beside it again. Max could see his smooth skin. His small flippers were curled up at the tips. He was using his tail to propel himself forward. "Hello, my friend," Max whispered to him.

Max realized that Sylvie had turned the boat. She was heading toward the small beach. Claude, Grandma and the Blancs had already arrived and were now waiting there. Sylvie slowed down as the water got more and more shallow. Gymmy was still beside them.

"OK, Sylvie," Dr. Leduc said. "I think I'd better do it now."

Sylvie drove close to shore and turned off the

motor. Dr. Leduc carefully stood up in the boat. He picked up the hoop net. The hoop was as wide around as a whale! A long net hung from the large hoop.

"Now hold on to the sides of the boat, everyone," Dr. Leduc said. He leaned out of the boat, held out the net and swiftly slipped it over Gymmy's head. Then Dr. Leduc jumped out of the boat and into the water. The cold water was up to his chest. Dr. Leduc held firmly to the net. He brought it over the whole front half of the beluga's body, including his fins.

Gymmy must be surprised! thought Max.

The whale stopped swimming as he felt the net holding him. Dr. Leduc stood steady in the river and gripped the net firmly. But how long could he hold the whale? Max wondered.

Then Claude waded out and tied the towrope around the thick part of Gymmy's tail.

"Well done," Dr. Leduc said. "Now let's move him into shallower water."

Max was amazed that Gymmy seemed so calm! He had his head in a net, but he wasn't thrashing about, trying to escape. He seemed to trust the people who so gently floated him through the water.

The motorboat touched the beach and Sylvie

hopped out and pulled it in. Max and Sarah climbed out.

Dr. Leduc called to Grandma and Claude. "Please bring the Zodiac raft, some buckets and the stretcher right down here to us. Quickly."

Grandma and Claude hurried up to the truck. In a moment, they had carried the inflatable raft, with the stretcher and buckets in it, down to the beach. They put the stretcher in the water, and Claude got in after it. He pulled it along until it floated alongside Gymmy.

"Our friend Gymmy wouldn't swim down the river by himself. So now we are going to give him a free ride, all expenses paid, to the St. Lawrence!" Dr. Leduc said with a smile. "We are going to put him in the stretcher, and then in the raft. Gymmy is going to lounge there while we tow him. Beth, could you please start filling the Zodiac with water to prepare it for our friend?"

"Of course," Grandma said, and began dipping the bucket into the water and pouring it into the raft.

"Claude and Sylvie, position yourselves, please." Dr. Leduc's two assistants moved to the other side of the whale. "Now, let's slip the stretcher underneath Gymmy," Dr. Leduc instructed.

Together, Claude, Sylvie and Dr. Leduc managed to slide the stretcher underneath the whale. Then Claude and Sylvie each took a set of handles, while Dr. Leduc went to the shore and pulled the Zodiac out to them. He positioned it at one end of the stretcher. Then he took a stretcher handle from Sylvie.

"Now, let's lift the stretcher onto the raft," said Dr. Leduc. "On the count of three. Are you ready? One . . . two . . . three!"

Dr. Leduc and Sylvie moved their end of the stretcher up and onto the raft while Claude pushed from behind. Finally, Gymmy was in the Zodiac. He lay there quietly, half covered in water.

Then Dr. Leduc climbed in. "OK, now we must continue to move quickly," he said. Claude handed him a black case and a bucket. Dr. Leduc found a spot for the case between his legs. "I'll be using the medical instruments in my bag to monitor Gymmy's heartbeat and his breathing. I'll check to see that he doesn't become too nervous or upset while we travel. If he does, we may have to release him right away – no matter where we are," he explained.

Max frowned. What if they had to release Gymmy *before* they got below the dam?

"I'll also be pouring water on him," Dr. Leduc added. He dipped his bucket over the side of the raft and poured water on Gymmy as he talked. "We must keep our friend as wet as possible," he told Max and Sarah. "If we do this, Gymmy will certainly be all right for a while. But it's not good for a whale to be out of the water for too long!"

Dr. Leduc looked at Mr. Blanc. "You are most familiar with this river, Pierre. Will you please tow the Zodiac with your little boat? We need to go below the dam, but it would be best to go even further, as close to the St. Lawrence River as possible."

Mr. Blanc beamed with pleasure. "Of course," he answered. Sylvie, Claude and Mr. Blanc went to get the boat ready.

Max watched as Dr. Leduc poured water over Gymmy, causing the whale's grey skin to glisten in the sunshine. But not all of his body was getting wet. "The water isn't reaching the area near Gymmy's head," she said to Dr. Leduc.

Sarah twirled her red braids anxiously. "His skin is dry there."

Dr. Leduc tugged at his beard. "And this is where I need to ask for your help one more time, girls," Dr. Leduc said. "I really need another person

— someone small, because there's not much room in here — to sit near Gymmy's head and pour water on it while we take him downriver. Would one of you volunteer to do this for him?"

Chapter 10

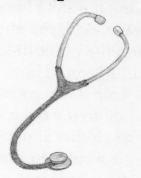

Start Pouring

Max looked at Sarah. Max knew how much her friend loved animals, and she knew how Sarah loved to care for them. She knew because she felt the same way! "You go, Sarah. You should go and help," Max offered.

But Sarah was already shaking her head. "No, Max," she said firmly. "Thanks, but I have had enough of boats for one day – really!"

Max was going to argue, but she knew they were in a rush. "OK," Max said. She turned to Dr. Leduc and a huge smile lit up her face. "I'd love to help."

"It won't be comfortable," he warned her. "There is another wet suit which should be small enough to fit you" – Claude held it up – "and it'll keep you somewhat warm, but it won't keep you dry. You'll be sitting in cold water, and you must keep pouring water on the beluga the whole time we are moving."

"I don't mind," Max told him. She was ready to do anything to help Gymmy survive. She and Grandma hurried up to the truck. Grandma helped Max slip out of her clothes and into the wet suit. It wasn't too loose; it would do fine. Then Max put her life jacket back on over top.

Grandma looked Max in the eyes. "Are you sure you want to do this?" she asked her.

Max nodded. At that moment, there wasn't anything else she wanted more.

Grandma must have seen that Max's mind was made up. "Okay, then. Do your best. And be careful," Grandma said.

Max and Grandma quickly returned to the beach.

"Good luck," Sarah told Max, smiling encouragingly, and handing her a bucket. Max waded into the water toward the raft. It was a strange feeling. Even with the wet suit on, she could feel the sharp cold of the river water through the protective layer.

Gymmy's eye followed her movements.

"Hello, fellow," Max said. "It's going to be OK," she reassured him. Max felt her heart pound with excitement. *Gymmy was so close!*

She scrambled into the water-filled, whale-filled raft, trying not to kick Gymmy. She sat down into cold water up to her waist.

As soon as she was settled, Dr. Leduc urged, "Please start pouring water on him right away. It's our task to keep him wet. But you must be careful not to let any water go down Gymmy's blowhole. To him, this would be like swallowing water."

"All right," Max said. "I'll do my best." She began filling her bucket from the pool of water at her feet.

"OK?" It was Mr. Blanc shouting from the aluminum boat.

"All set! Let's go," Dr. Leduc shouted back.

Max heard the engine of the boat start up. She looked toward shore. Sarah waved to her, then clasped both hands together and shook them in the air, cheering her on. Max smiled back, encouraged. She lifted the bucket, and as she poured the water over Gymmy's head and back, she felt the gentle tug of the rope. The raft was moving.

Would Gymmy panic? Would he flip and flop and end up stuck here, still trapped above the dam?

Max gently placed her wet-gloved hand on the whale's forehead. She looked into his eyes. He looked back at her calmly, as if he knew that she was trying to help him. "It'll be all right," Max told him again.

As Mr. Blanc steered the boat and the raft through the sandbars, Max poured water over Gymmy. And as they passed through the sandbars and then headed downstream, Max continued to pour water over Gymmy.

Dr. Leduc poured water too. Every once in a while, he used a stethoscope to listen to Gymmy's heart rate and his breathing. Each time, he would turn to Max and give her a thumbs-up.

It gave Max an incredible feeling to be so close to an animal that lived underwater. She marvelled at the whale's thick, rubbery skin. She tried to spot Gymmy's ears, which she knew were behind his eyes, but only the size of a pinprick. She gazed at the large "melon" that bulged over his beak.

As they rode on and on, Max's arms started to ache from lifting the bucket of water. Her legs and feet were freezing cold. But not for a moment did she think about quitting. Stay calm, she silently told the whale. Stay calm.

And then, finally, she saw that they were approaching the dam. There were workers in construction hats busy along the shore. Max saw them stop and lift their heads to watch them chug past.

She felt the river catch the inflatable raft and sweep them forward, as the water flowed through the narrow space between two steel beams.

And then they were out the other side.

Chapter 11

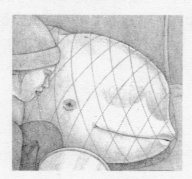

One, Two, Three!

A huge grin spread across Max's face. "Gymmy!" she cried, touching the beluga's damp neck. "We made it. You're through! We got past in time!"

Cheering erupted from the motorboat. Mr. Blanc, Claude and Sylvie waved their arms in the air.

Once they were well downstream, Mr. Blanc shut off the motor so they could talk. "Where is a good place to stop, Dr. Leduc?" he asked.

"We want to get Gymmy back in the water soon," Dr. Leduc said. "But it would be best to get him as close to the mouth of the river as possible. That way we know that Gymmy won't try to head back up the river again. We want to make sure that he heads out into the St. Lawrence where he can join the other belugas."

Mr. Blanc tugged on the cord and the engine started up. The journey down the river continued.

Max's shoulders were aching. She began switching sides to ease the effort, lifting the bucket first with her right arm, then her left.

Gymmy was still calm. His creases and folds of fat rose and fell as he breathed. Max could only see the flipper on the side of the whale nearest her. It lay still. Only the blinking of Gymmy's eye told Max that he was very much awake, and very alert.

Gymmy was so large. He was longer than the height of Dr. Leduc, and only half grown. Max imagined him swimming in the wide St. Lawrence, chasing fish along the bottom of the river. She pictured him diving and spyhopping with other belugas, growing and becoming an adult. It brought a smile to her face.

Max poured more water over the whale's head, holding one hand over his blowhole to keep it clear. She could picture Gymmy free — but she was still uneasy. He had been in the inflatable raft for a long time. How long could a whale be out of water and still all right?

Just then, Dr. Leduc called out. He was pointing ahead, and he looked pleased. Max saw that the river was widening. In fact, it was widening a lot. This must be the mouth, where St. Paul's River joined the St. Lawrence.

"You're almost home, Gymmy!" Max told the whale.

Mr. Blanc began to circle a small island. He pointed the nose of the boat toward the beach and headed in. Soon the motorboat was bumping up on the shore. Claude and Sylvie jumped out and gently pulled on the towrope. The raft and its passengers were now floating in shallow water.

"Excellent, excellent," Dr. Leduc cried. "Now there's no time to waste. Let's say goodbye to our young traveller and send him on his way!

"We'll move Gymmy by lifting him in the stretcher over the side of the raft," Dr. Leduc instructed. "Max and I will remain in the Zodiac and lift from here. On the count of three. One, two, three!"

Max patted the whale's rubbery neck. Then she reached for a stretcher handle. She gazed into Gymmy's eye as she helped lift him out into the shallow water.

"Now we'll move him into deeper water," Dr.

Leduc said. He and Max climbed out of the Zodiac and helped slide the stretcher from under the whale. Claude removed the rope from Gymmy's tail. Then Dr. Leduc used the hoop net to guide Gymmy forward, while the others gently pushed him along with their hands.

When the water reached Max's chest, Dr. Leduc said, "OK, this is deep enough."

With one slow and careful movement, Dr. Leduc slipped the hoop net forward, away from Gymmy's body and off his head. Now there was nothing holding Gymmy there. He was surrounded only by the people who had cared for him.

Claude said goodbye to the whale and moved away. Then Sylvie and Dr. Leduc did the same, each giving the whale a pat before turning to wade back to shore.

Only Max was left beside him. Gymmy turned his head this way and that. Max guessed that he was using his sonar to check out where he was. For the last time, she reached out and touched the whale's back.

"Go, Gymmy. Go to the deep, wide river, and don't come back up here again!"

Gymmy turned his head once more. He seemed to look straight into Max's eyes, and the whale and

67

the girl shared a grin of friendship. Then Gymmy swam away. He headed straight out toward the mouth of the river, where it ran into the St. Lawrence.

Max stood and watched, the cold water numbing her legs and arms. She saw him surface for air once, and then disappear below the water.

And that was all. The baby beluga whale was gone.

"Hurrah! Hurrah!" It was Sarah, Grandma and Mrs. Blanc. They had driven down the shore road beside St. Paul's River, hoping to watch Gymmy's release. They had arrived just in time.

When the rescuers landed back on shore, Grandma took one look at her wet, cold, thrilled granddaughter and quickly bundled her into the car to change into dry clothes. "Good work, Max," Grandma said. "Now we're heading back to the Blancs' so you can have a warm bath and a hot lunch."

Sarah snuggled into the back seat next to her. "Oh, Max, you did it! You did it! And now you have to tell me everything — absolutely everything — about the trip downriver!"

Max started right from the beginning. She told her friend how wonderful it had felt to sit next to

Gymmy, and how nervous she had been about keeping him wet and healthy. She shared how relieved she had been when they'd passed through the dam.

Sarah listened, wide-eyed. "What an adventure we've had," she sighed.

As the car drove back along the shore, Max looked out at the water. Yes, she had really helped rescue a beluga whale. She remembered the feel of Gymmy's skin under her gloved hand. She thought about his eyes meeting hers. There had been a spark of something shared. She was sure of it. And then there had been the whale's grin, matching hers.

It was wonderful that the whale had reached the St. Lawrence. But Max knew that the beluga had troubles to face there, too. The noise of the boats, the pollution of the river . . . Max sighed. She and Sarah had helped Gymmy today, but maybe there was *more* they could do.

She thought for a moment. Then suddenly, she had an idea. At Wild Paws and Claws Clinic and Rehabilitation Centre, they mainly looked after forest animals. But Wild Paws and Claws was all about returning animals back to the wild – just as they had done today. She and Sarah could post information about belugas there, so visitors could learn more about them and their watery world.

Max sighed once more, content and drowsy. She closed her eyes and saw again the young beluga back in the water. He was out of the netting, swimming away, home again. Max smiled happily. Yes, the baby beluga was free.

Beluga Information Sheet

🐾 Beluga whales live in arctic and subarctic water all around the polar seas. They are found in the waters of Alaska, Norway, Greenland, Russia and Canada. Belugas belong to the family of white whales. Their closest relative is the narwhal.

🐾 Belugas mate in spring or early summer. After fourteen months, single calves are born. They stay with their mother for about two years. Belugas live in pods of two or three or more — even in groups of hundreds! Belugas can live to be more than 35 years old.

🐾 Some beluga populations migrate — they travel to warmer waters in winter, and cooler waters in summer. Others, such as the St. Lawrence River belugas, stay in one area year-round.

🐾 A beluga whale needs about 12 kg of food — such as salmon, cod, shrimp, char and octopus — each day.

❀ Belugas can move their foreheads and mouths, changing the expressions on their faces. Sometimes they look like they are smiling, frowning or even whistling!

❀ Belugas have few natural enemies. Northern belugas are hunted by killer whales, polar bears and man. In some Inuit communities, belugas are still a very important source of meat and fuel.

❀ Belugas in the St. Lawrence River are listed as endangered by the Committee on the Status of Endangered Wildlife. They have been legally protected since 1983. They are no longer hunted, but this does not mean they are out of danger. Belugas have been seriously harmed by toxic chemicals from factories. Now there is an action plan in place to reduce industrial pollution in the river.

❀ Belugas rely on echolocation (they use sound to "see" objects) to catch their prey and find their way around underwater. But in the busy St. Lawrence

River, the noise from industry and whale-watching boats interferes with echolocation. This is another reason why the belugas there are endangered.